Written by Lynne Gibbs
Illustrated by Rachael O'Neill

Published by Brimax,
A division of Autumn Publishing Group
© 2004 Autumn Publishing Limited
Appledram Barns, Chichester PO20 7EQ

ISBN 1-85854-903-5 (Hardback)

Printed in China

A CIP catalogue record for this book is available from the British Library.

Poems for Babies

BRIMAX

A baby's tears

Playing around in your bath,
You giggle and wriggle and laugh.
Then you frown and start to cry,
As water splashes in your eye.

Suddenly you look at me.
You're happy again, I can see.
You wave your arms in the air,
Splashing water everywhere.

A perfect smile

Ten tiny fingers,
Ten tiny toes.

A perfect smile,
And a button nose.

Skin so soft,
Eyes so blue.

Who could I mean?
It has to be you!

Sweet dreams

It's time for bed,
So close your eyes.
No more tears,
No more sighs.

Dream of all things
Happy and bright.
Stay warm and snug
Until it's light.

So special

How many times do I tell you,
That I love you more each day?
But it's true, you know,
I really do, in a very special way!

Every little step you take,
Every smile I see,
Makes my heart beat faster,
Because you belong to me!

Time passes

Soon you will be walking,
Running and talking.
Soon you will be going to school.

Soon you will be dating
And no longer waiting
For me to help you to crawl.

But until that day's here,
I'll treasure you, dear
And take care of you every day.

Together we will walk,
Together we will talk,
And I'll help you all the way.

You're amazing!

I catch my breath
When I look at you.

It's quite amazing
The things you can do.

You know who I am,
You hear what I say.

You learn something new
Almost every day.

True love

Already you have taught me,
So many special things.
You've shown me what true love is
And the happiness it brings.

How can a little baby
Make such a change in me?
Now you never hear me say just 'I',
It's always 'us' and 'we'.

Busy bee!

Running around, preparing your meals,
Only I know how it feels!

Then just as I think you've gone to sleep,
You let out a cry and begin to weep.

I'm always busy, night and day.
You want a cuddle, you want to play!

Leaving all my tasks undone,
Over to you, sweet baby, I run.

My wishes for you

It seems in just a blink of an eye,
So much time has passed us by.
Was it really that long ago,
In my tummy I felt you grow?

All the dreams I have for you,
I will try to make come true!
But whatever you grow up to be,
Just be happy, healthy - and free!

As you dream

It's time to wake - get out of bed.
You really are a sleepyhead!

I watch you as you lie and dream
And wonder what those faces mean.

What do you dream of lying there,
Without a worry, or a care?

Simple thoughts fill your mind,
A baby's dream - the sweetest kind.

Each new day!

You press and pull
At a toy you've found.
Your eyes open wide,
And you look around.

What could this be?
You seem to say.
You'll see many more 'firsts'
With each new day!

Special feelings

The day you were born,
Was a special day.
It changed our lives,
In every way.

We didn't mind having
A girl or a boy,
For whatever you were,
Would bring such joy.

But we never imagined
Feelings quite so strong.
Oh, sweet little baby,
You can do no wrong.